Mixed-Up Dollhouse

Adapted by Violet Zhang

ISBN 978-1-338-64169-1

10 9 8 7 6 5 4 3 2 1   21 22 23 24 25

Printed in the U.S.A.   40

First printing 2021

Book design by Salena Mahina

Scholastic Inc.

Gabby pulled a cat-tastic Dollhouse Delivery from her Meow Meow Mailbox. It was a glitter globe with the Dollhouse inside! But wait a minute . . .

This Dollhouse was all mixed up! The roof was on the bottom, the ears were on the side . . . and when Gabby shook the glitter globe, silly sounds came out.

"Sounds like it's broken," said Gabby.

When she looked at the *real* Dollhouse, she saw that it was all mixed up, too. MerCat and her bathtub were in the music room. "That doesn't belong there!" said Gabby.

"We'd better get in there and fix this," Gabby said to Pandy. "Time to get tiny!" She put on her magical headband and sang her special "pinch pinch" song to take them into the Dollhouse.

Inside the music room, MerCat was upset.

"Thank goodness you're here!" she said. "I was getting ready to take a bath when I heard these silly sounds. Then. . .poof! I'm in the wrong room!"

DJ Catnip strolled in, playing a groovy tune. He stopped when he saw the bathtub.

"A bathtub in the music room?" he said. "This is kind of funky."

"I think I know what happened," Gabby explained. "I shook this glitter globe and made the Dollhouse all mixed up!"

"Oh no! How are we going to fix it?" Pandy asked.

"Don't worry, Pandy! We don't know how to fix it . . . yet! Maybe we can lift the tub and bring it back to the bathroom!" said Gabby. They tried lifting the tub, but it was too heavy.

"Sometimes, a little music helps me come up with new ideas," said DJ Catnip. He picked up his tuba and started to play.

"Ooh! That's a bubbly little tune," said MerCat. "I like it!" That gave her an idea!

"We can solve this problem with a little spa science," MerCat said. She pulled something from her pocket. "My travel bubbles!" she said.

With DJ Catnip's permission, MerCat blew some bubbles into his tuba.

This time when he played, huge bubbles came out!

The bubbles stuck to the side of the bathtub. Gabby and Pandy hopped in with MerCat. The bubbles began lifting them off the ground.

"We're floating!" said Gabby.

"PAW-SOME!" said Pandy. They floated all the way back to the bathroom!

Back in the music room, CatRat popped up. He had followed the sound of DJ Catnip's tune.

"Oh hey," said DJ Catnip. "I was just playing something to help the bathtub fly back up to the bathroom. Catch you later!"

Just then, something sparkly caught CatRat's eye. It was the glitter globe with the mixed-up Dollhouse! Gabby accidentally left it there.

"Ooh, shiny is miney," said CatRat.

Meanwhile, in the Dollhouse kitchen, Cakey Cat was decorating cookies.

"Sprinkle, sprinkle, sprinkle!" he sang.

While Cakey was singing, CatRat walked in. "Just passing through," he said.

As he walked, CatRat gave the glitter globe a closer look. "I think this thing is broken," he said. He gave it a shake as he left the kitchen.

Gabby and Pandy rushed into the kitchen and blew all the sprinkles off of Cakey. He explained, "CatRat came by with a glitter globe and then I heard all kinds of silly sounds."

"Uh-oh," said Gabby. "CatRat must have found the mixed-up glitter globe and shook it up. We'll find him, but first let's help you get this place clean!"

They swept the sprinkles into a giant pile. Using her magic headband, Gabby pinched her ear to cover the walls in a fun cookie pattern. They all took a deep breath and blew. The sprinkles flew onto every cookie.

"So sparkly!" said Cakey.

Gabby and Pandy left Cakey to find CatRat. They heard a sound from the craft room. When they entered, they found . . . CraftRat! "Somebody's got to fix me," he cried.

Baby Box pointed to the glitter globe. "He shook that thing!" she said.

"Hmm, maybe if we fix the mixed-up glitter globe, we can fix CatRat," said Gabby.

"That's a crafty-rific idea!" said Baby Box. She took apart the glitter globe and rolled out a blueprint of the Dollhouse.

"We just have to match the pieces," she said.

"Like a puzzle!" said Pandy.

Piece by piece, they put the mixed-up Dollhouse back together. But CatRat was still CraftRat.

"I think we need to do one more thing," said Gabby. "Everybody say, 'Shake, shake, shake!'"

CatRat was back to normal!

"I'm me again!" he said. "Oh, I missed me. Thanks, Gabby Cats."

With everyone in the room together, Pandy shook the glitter globe one last time.

"Meow-mazing," everyone said as glitter fell from above.

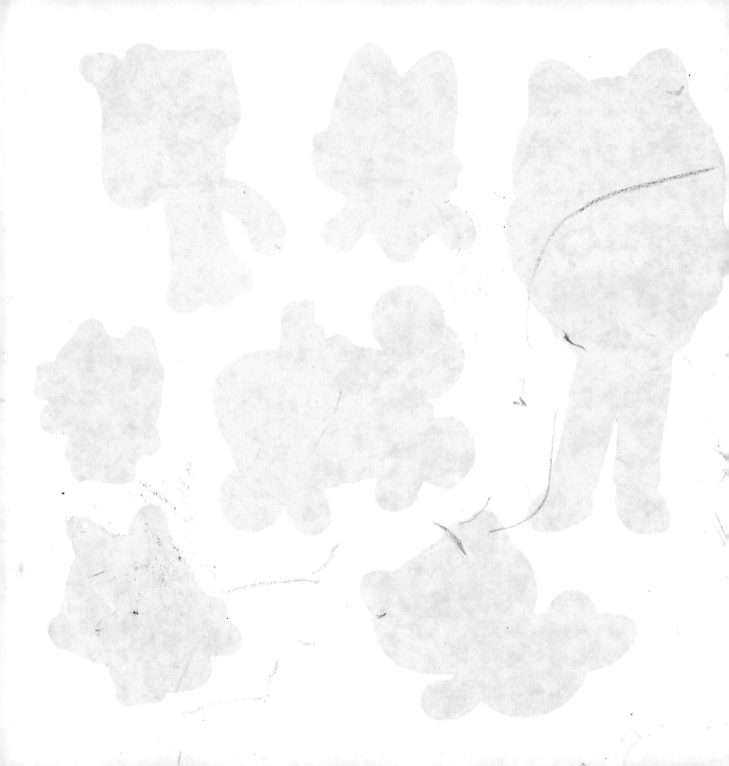

Sprinkle party!

Decorate these **CAT-TASTIC** postcards!

You're a **PURR-IFIC FRIEND!**